NEW PATCHES FOR OLD

A Turkish Folktale Retold by Barbara K. Walker
& Ahmet E. Uysal Illustrated by Harold Berson

Parents' Magazine Press/New York

Text copyright © 1974 by Barbara K. Walker
Illustrations copyright © 1974 by Harold Berson
Printed in the United States of America

Library of Congress Cataloging in Publications Data

Walker, Barbara K.
    New patches for old.
    SUMMARY: Hasan needs his new trousers shortened,
but neither his wife, mother, nor daughter has time to
do it—at first.
    [1. Folklore—Turkey] I. Uysal, Ahmet E., joint
author. II. Berson, Harold, illus. III. Title.
PZ8.1.W128Ne   398.2'2'09561   [E]   73–12951
ISBN 0–8193–0713–0
ISBN 0–8193–0714–9 (lib. bdg.)

*For Jane and Julie Curl
and our drugstore ghost*

One day, Hasan the Shoemaker closed his shop a bit early. "Tomorrow evening the holidays begin," he said. "I'll buy something new for my family."

For his wife he
bought a blouse.

For his mother he bought a scarf.

And for his married
daughter he bought four
bright hair ribbons.

Then, looking down at his own
clothes, he said, "I must buy
a new pair of trousers for myself.
These old ones are just patches
on patches."

He hurried to the tailor's shop. "Have you trousers to fit me?" he asked.

"See for yourself," said the tailor. "I have only one pair left."

Hasan held that pair up against his old ones. "They seem all right around the waist," he said, "but they're three fingers too long. Can you shorten them?"

"Not today," said the tailor. "Ask your wife to shorten them."

"All right," said Hasan. He paid the tailor and hastened home with his parcels.

His wife liked her blouse. "How fine!" she said.
"And what did *you* get?"

"I bought these trousers," Hasan answered, "but
they're three fingers too long. Could you shorten
them?"

"Not now," she said. "I want to sew sequins on
my new blouse. Why not ask your mother? She
does everything so well!"

"All right," said Hasan, and along he went to his mother's house. "Mother," he said, "I've bought you a new scarf for the holidays."

"How fine!" she said. "And what did you buy for yourself?"

"These trousers," he answered, "but they're three fingers too long. Could you shorten them?"

"Son, I have no time for sewing.
The holidays begin tomorrow,
and I must pray for our dead relatives.
Why not ask your daughter? She
should be good for *something*."
"All right," Hasan said, and along
he went to his daughter's house.

"Daughter," he said, "I've bought you some ribbons for the holidays."

"How fine!" said his daughter. "And what did you buy for yourself?"

"These trousers," he answered, "but they're three fingers too long. Could you shorten them?"

"Oh, no, Father!" she said. "I must feed the baby, and then I'll iron my ribbons. Surely my mother or your mother will shorten them."

Hasan thought and thought. Then he hurried to his shop. Carefully he cut a piece three fingers wide from the end of each trouser leg. With his big shoemaker's needle he put new hems in the trousers. Then, folding them over his arm, he went along home and put them on his shelf.

The next afternoon, Hasan closed his shop very early.
Nodding to this one and smiling at that one, he
strolled home. Everyone was feeling the happiness
of the holidays.

His wife met him at the door. "Come in," she said.
"Your mother and our daughter are here."
Hasan was surprised. His mother? His daughter?
Hasan's mother looked lovely in her new scarf.
"As soon as you're ready, Son, we'll all go to the
festival together," she said. Then she smiled.
She had a secret.

"Husband, *do* be quick," said his wife. "Put on those new trousers. See? I am wearing my new blouse." She was smiling to herself, for she had a fine secret.

And, "Please, Father, don't be long," urged his
daughter, with her new ribbons blooming in her hair.
She, too, was smiling about a secret of her own.
Ah, they are all fine-looking women, thought Hasan,
even if they hadn't had the time to do the sewing.
He would be pleased to take them with him to the festival.

And he went into the bedroom to put on his new trousers, trousers exactly right around the waist *and* exactly the right length. He ought to know, for hadn't he shortened them himself?

Suddenly, "Eh vah!" cried Hasan.

"Are you sick?" called his wife.

"No—oh, no. But something has happened to my trousers!" And opening the door, he stood there to show them what he meant.

His fine new trousers
hung just below his knees.

Hasan's wife and Hasan's mother and Hasan's daughter all said, "But I shortened them only three fingers!" Then, realizing what must have happened, they stared at Hasan.

As for Hasan, he stared back at them, too stunned to speak.

"My dear," said his wife, "last night while you were out visiting your friends, I remembered the trousers. 'He's such a good husband,' I said to myself. 'I'll shorten the trousers while he's gone.' There was *such* a clumsy hem at the bottom of each leg! But I ripped out the hems and cut exactly three fingers off the ends. Then I hemmed them neatly and put them back on your shelf."

Hasan's mother smiled ruefully. "I came this morning after your wife had gone to do her marketing. I had finished my prayers, and I said to myself, 'Hasan is such a good son. I'll shorten his trousers now.' I found the trousers and let down the hems and cut a piece exactly three fingers' width from the end of each leg. I made neat hems in them and put them on your shelf. I wanted to surprise you!"

"Oh, you did, Mother!" Hasan said, smiling despite
himself.

Then it was his daughter's turn. "Father, I was
rocking my baby this morning when I remembered
your trousers. 'He's such a kind father,' I
said to myself. 'I *must* shorten his trousers.'
So I bundled up the baby and hurried over here.
I found the trousers on your shelf and took out
the hems and trimmed three fingers' width from
each leg and put in new hems.

Then I folded the trousers and put them back on
your shelf and took the baby along home. I wanted
it to be a nice surprise for you."

Hasan looked from one to the other. Then he laughed. "But I had already shortened them myself!"

"You?" they exclaimed.

"Yes. Someone had to do it, so I cut off the ends and hemmed them up myself."

Suddenly they all shouted with laughter. And, in
the middle of their laughing, they thought what
they could do; they could sew all the pieces back
onto the trousers. As Allah would have it, when
they had finished, the trousers were exactly the
right length.

"Well, my dears," said Hasan, "at least all my patches are *new* patches!" And, dressed in their holiday finery, away they went to the festival.

Barbara K. Walker was born in Michigan, grew up in New York, and now lives in Lubbock, Texas. Her husband, Warren Walker, was a Fulbright lecturer at Ankara University, and the year they spent in Turkey gave the Walkers an opportunity to study the Turkish people and their folklore. Now, in collaboration with Ahmet E. Uysal, they have collected over 1,500 Turkish folktales. The collection is to be called the Uysal-Walker Archive of Turkish Oral Narrative and housed at the Texas Tech University Library. Mrs. Walker has re-told many folktales from various countries, and she is represented on the Parents' Magazine Press list by *Watermelons, Walnuts and the Wisdom of Allah* (a collection of 18 Turkish tales), *How the Hare Told the Truth About his Horse, The Round Sultan and the Straight Answer,* and *The Dancing Palmtree and Other Nigerian Folktales.*

Ahmet E. Uysal was born in a small village in Turkey and is now a professor in the Department of English at the University of An-kara. He is the author of many articles and books for adults. How-ever, this is his first book for children. He discovered the tale, *Trousers Too Long and Too Short* (retold here as *New Patches for Old*) in a village in southwest Turkey.

Harold Berson studied art in Paris and later graduated from U.C.L.A. where he majored in sociology. Like Barbara Walker, he has traveled extensively. He and his wife Paula, also an artist, have toured France, Morocco, Yugoslavia and Greece as well as Turkey, spending most of their time drawing and painting. Mr. Berson has also illustrated for Parents' Magazine Press *The King and the Whirlybird, The Pelican Chorus, Watermelons, Walnuts and the Wisdom of Allah,* and *Ittki Pittki.* When not traveling, the Bersons make their home in New York City.